STEP INTO READING®

1

STEP

READY TO READ

GO, GO, TRUCKS!

by Jennifer Liberts

illustrated by Mike Yamada

Random House 🏠 New York

Red truck.

Dear Parents:

Congratulations! Your child is taking the first steps on an exciting journey. The destination? Independent reading!

STEP INTO READING® will help your child get there. The program offers five steps to reading success. Each step includes fun stories and colorful art or photographs. In addition to original fiction and books with favorite characters, there are Step into Reading Non-Fiction Readers, Phonics Readers and Boxed Sets, Sticker Readers, and Comic Readers—a complete literacy program with something to interest every child.

Learning to Read, Step by Step!

Ready to Read   Preschool–Kindergarten
• big type and easy words • rhyme and rhythm • picture clues
For children who know the alphabet and are eager to begin reading.

Reading with Help   Preschool–Grade 1
• basic vocabulary • short sentences • simple stories
For children who recognize familiar words and sound out new words with help.

Reading on Your Own   Grades 1–3
• engaging characters • easy-to-follow plots • popular topics
For children who are ready to read on their own.

Reading Paragraphs   Grades 2–3
• challenging vocabulary • short paragraphs • exciting stories
For newly independent readers who read simple sentences with confidence.

Ready for Chapters   Grades 2–4
• chapters • longer paragraphs • full-color art
For children who want to take the plunge into chapter books but still like colorful pictures.

STEP INTO READING® is designed to give every child a successful reading experience. The grade levels are only guides; children will progress through the steps at their own speed, developing confidence in their reading. The F&P Text Level on the back cover serves as another tool to help you choose the right book for your child.

Remember, a lifetime love of reading starts with a single step!

To Harriet Horowitz—
thank you for encouraging my love
of writing in the fifth grade.
—J.L.

Text copyright © 2017 by Jennifer Liberts
Cover art and interior illustrations copyright © 2017 by Mike Yamada

Visit us on the Web!
StepIntoReading.com
randomhousekids.com

Educators and librarians, for a variety of teaching tools,
visit us at RHTeachersLibrarians.com

Library of Congress Cataloging-in-Publication Data is available upon request.
ISBN 978-0-399-54951-9 (trade) — ISBN 978-0-399-54952-6 (lib. bdg.) —
ISBN 978-0-399-54953-3 (ebook)

Printed in the United States of America
10 9 8 7 6 5
First Edition

This book has been officially leveled by using the F&P Text Level Gradient™ Leveling System.

Green truck.

Great big wheels truck.

Old truck.

New truck.

Yummy food truck!

Garbage trucks

to truck the yuck.

Big dump trucks

to dump the muck!

Small trucks,
smaller trucks,
in a row.

Kids make small trucks
go, go, go!

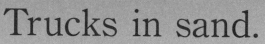

Trucks in sand.

Trucks in dirt.

Trucks in snow.

Blow, truck. Blow!

Time for a ride.

Get inside!

One rig.

Two rigs.

Three rigs.

Four!

Big truck,
bigger truck!

We want more!

Shiny red fire truck—

honk, honk, honk!

Trucks in mud.

Trucks get stuck!

Right side up.

Upside down.

Trucks, trucks, trucks are all around!